This Little Tiger book belongs to:

_____

_____

_____

For Sue and Paul
~ A H B

For Jess
~ T W

LITTLE TIGER PRESS
1 The Coda Centre, 189 Munster Road, London SW6 6AW
www.littletiger.co.uk

First published in Great Britain 1998
This edition published 2014 by Little Tiger Press, London
Text copyright © A.H. Benjamin 1998
Illustrations copyright © Tim Warnes 1998
Visit Tim Warnes at www.ChapmanandWarnes.com
A.H. Benjamin and Tim Warnes have asserted their rights
to be identified as the author and illustrator of this work
under the Copyright, Designs and Patents Act, 1988

Printed in China • LTP/1900/0814/1013
10 9 8 7 6 5 4 3 2 1

IT COULD HAVE BEEN WORSE...

A.H. Benjamin   Tim Warnes

LITTLE TIGER PRESS

Mouse was on his way back home
after visiting his town cousin,
when . . .

WHOOPS!

...he lost his balance
and fell to the ground.

"Ouch!" said Mouse. "This isn't my lucky day."

But it could have been worse!

Mouse picked himself up
and carried on his way.
He came to an open field
and was scurrying across it,
when . . .

CRASH!

...he fell into a dark hole.

"Why do things *always* go wrong for me?" grumbled Mouse.

But it could have been worse!

Mouse clambered out of the
hole and was off again.

"I think I'll take a rest," he said.
Mouse had just found a comfortable spot,
when . . .

OUCH!

...he sat on a thistle
and shot into the air.

"Everything bad happens to me!" wailed Mouse as he pulled some thorns out of his bottom.

But it could have been worse!

Mouse walked down the hill until
he reached a stream. He began to
cross it by stepping on the stones,
when . . .

"I'm so cold and wet!"
complained Mouse.

But it could have been worse!

Mouse paddled to the edge of the
stream and climbed out of the water.

Shaking himself dry, he was just about to scramble down a steep bank, when . . .

WHEEE!

...he lost his footing and skidded right to the bottom.

"I'll be black and blue all over," cried Mouse.

But it could have been worse!

Mouse staggered to his feet
and ran all the way home.

"It's been a terrible day," he said to his mother as she bathed his cuts and bruises. "I fell into a hole, got wet in the river, and—"
"Never mind, Son," his mother said . . .